AMAZING WORLD OF

SHARKS

Written by Cynthia Stierle

Reviewed by Mystic Aquarium, Fish & Invertebrates, Aquarist Team

Silver Dolphin

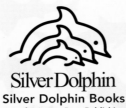

Silver Dolphin Books

An imprint of Printers Row Publishing Group
A division of Readerlink Distribution Services, LLC
10350 Barnes Canyon Road, Suite 100, San Diego, CA 92121
www.silverdolphinbooks.com

Printers Row Publishing Group is a division of Readerlink Distribution Services, LLC.
Silver Dolphin Books is a registered trademark of Readerlink Distribution Services, LLC.

All notations of errors or omissions should be addressed to
Silver Dolphin Books, Editorial Department, at the above address.

A component of ISBN 978-1-68412-602-6. Not for individual sale.

Manufactured, printed, and assembled in Shenzhen, China.
First printing, August 2018. HH/08/18

22 21 20 19 18   1 2 3 4 5

ART AND PHOTOGRAPHY CREDITS
(t = top, b = bottom, l = left, r = right, c = center)

Front Cover: Roger Swainston (blue shark and sawshark); Marc Dando/Wildlife Art Ltd. (hammerhead);
Back Cover: ©Matt9122/shutterstock.com

Title Page: Ian Jackson/Wildlife Art Ltd.; Marc Dando/Wildlife Art Ltd.(b); Roger Swainston(cr); Ian Jackson/Wildlife Art Ltd;
Page 4: ©Willyam Bradberry/shutterstock.com; **Page 5:** ©mj007/shutterstock.com(t); Marc Dando/Wildlife Art Ltd.(cl);
Roger Swainston(cr); **Page 6:** ©stockpix4u/shutterstock.com; **Page 6 & 7:** Ray Grinaway; **Page 8:** ©Jim Agronick/shutterstock.com;
Page 9: ©Ian Scott/shutterstock.com; **Page 10:** Martin Camm; **Page 11:** ©Luiz Felipe V. Puntel/shutterstock.com (l);
Marc Dando/Wildlife Art Ltd.(r); **Page 12:** ©Sergey Uryadnikov/shutterstock.com; **Page 13:** ©BW Folsom/shutterstock.com (t);
©Joe Belanger/shutterstock.com (cl); ©Yulia_B/shutterstock.com (bl); ©NatalieJean/shutterstock.com (br);
Page 14: ©Fiona Ayerst/shutterstock.com (bl); ©Michael Bogner/shutterstock.com (bc); ©nicolas.voisin44/shutterstock.com (br);
Page 15: Roger Swainston; **Page 16:** Marc Dando/Wildlife Art Ltd.; **Page 17:** ©Ethan Daniels/shutterstock.com (t);
©Luiz Felipe V. Puntel/shutterstock.com (b); **Page 18:** ©Cigdem Sean Cooper/shutterstock.com; **Page 18 & 19:** Ian Jackson/Wildlife Art Ltd;
Page 19: ©John A. Anderson/shutterstock.com(b); **Page 20:** ©Jill Lang/shutterstock.com; **Page 21:** Chris Turnbull/Wildlife Art Ltd.;
Page 22: ©MidoSemsem/shutterstock.com(t); ©frantisekhojdysz/shutterstock.com (b); **Page 23:** ©Jung Hsuan/shutterstock.com (t);
©cbpix/shutterstock.com (b); **Page 24 & 25:** Roger Swainston; **Page 25:** Marc Dando/Wildlife Art Ltd.(t);
Page 26: Marc Dando/Wildlife Art Ltd.; **Page 27:** ©Matt9122/shutterstock.com(t); ©Shane Gross/shutterstock.com(b);
Page 28: ©Doptis/shutterstock.com; **Page 29:** ©JULIE LUCHT/shutterstock.com(t); Ian Jackson/Wildlife Art Ltd.(b);
Page 30: © kaschibo/shutterstock.com; **Page 31:** © Dudarev Mikhail/shutterstock.com(t); Martin Camm(b);
Page 32 & 33: Roger Swainston; **Page 34:** Roger Swainston(l, rb); Ian Jackson/Wildlife Art Ltd.(rt);
Page 35: ©PawelG Photo/shutterstock.com(t); Ian Jackson/Wildlife Art Ltd.(b); **Page 37:** Ian Jackson/Wildlife Art Ltd.

Diorama Imagery: ©Vilainecrevette/shutterstock.com; ©littlesam/shutterstock.com; ©Paweł Borówka/shutterstock.com;
©John A. Anderson/shutterstock.com; ©Ethan Daniels/shutterstock.com; ©Jolanta Wojcicka/shutterstock.com.

Stickers: ©Ian Scott/shutterstock.com; ©A Cotton Photo/shutterstock.com;
©J. Henning Buchholz/shutterstock.com; ©Kletr/shutterstock.com; ©Amanda Nicholls/shutterstock.com;
©Jim Agronick/shutterstock.com; ©Rich Carey/shutterstock.com; ©Boris Pamikov/shutterstock.com;
©bluehand/shutterstock.com; ©Lenor Ko/shutterstock.com; ©Narchuk/shutterstock.com;
©Richard Whitcombe/shutterstock.com; ©Polly Dawson/shutterstock.com; ©orlandin/shutterstock.com;
©Matt9122/shutterstock.com; ©ShaunWilkinson/shutterstock.com; ©aquapix/shutterstock.com;
©frantisekhojdysz/shutterstock.com; ©Joe Belanger/shutterstock.com; ©LauraD/shutterstock.com;
©IrinaK/shutterstock.com; ©Vilainecrevette/shutterstock.com.

Models: ©Sergey Uryadnikov/shutterstock.com, ©Vadim Petrakov/shutterstock.com (great white);
©Shane Gross/shutterstock.com, ©Matt9122/shutterstock.com (hammerhead); ©Ethan Daniels/shutterstock.com,
©kaschibo/shutterstock.com, ©Rich Carey/shutterstock.com (whale shark); ©Stubblefield Photography/shutterstock.com,
©Ethan Daniels/shutterstock.com, ©nicolas.voisin44/shutterstock.com, ©haveseen/shutterstock.com (manta ray).

General Backgrounds and Patterns: ©Nebojsa Kontic/shutterstock.com; ©oriontrail/shutterstock.com

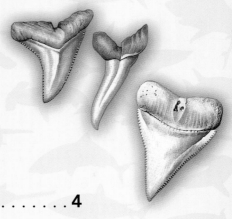

CONTENTS

WHAT ARE SHARKS?

What are the most fearsomely fascinating fish in the sea? If you said sharks, you're not alone. While many people think all sharks are large (and dangerous) creatures, about two-thirds of the more than 400 **species** of sharks are actually smaller than a skateboard. In fact, the tiny dwarf lantern shark can fit in the palm of your hand.

Where do sharks live and what do they eat? That depends on the species of shark. These top **predators** are found in all the world's oceans, from cold Arctic seas to warm tropical waters. Some hunt seals, while others gobble fish or crunch crabs. Whale sharks can grow to more than 40 feet long and are the largest fish in the sea, but they eat tiny creatures such as **plankton**.

Ready to meet these mysterious creatures? Let's dive in!

WHAT'S THAT WORD?

As you read, you will see words that are in **bold**. Look for them in the glossary on pages 36–37 to learn what they mean.

Megalodon tooth

BACK IN TIME

Megalodon is an extinct shark that roamed the seas more than 1.5 million years ago. Its teeth were about seven inches long!

Sawshark

Hammerhead shark

Angel shark

SHARK SHOWCASE

Think all sharks look the same? Think again! Angel sharks have flattened bodies to help them hide on the ocean floor. Sawsharks are equipped with toothy snouts to slash **prey**. The specially shaped heads of hammerhead sharks let them detect prey buried under the sand.

SUPER SENSES

The ocean is a big place, and its waters can be dark or murky. Finding food isn't easy. But sharks have survived for millions of years because their senses are **adapted** for hunting in the sea.

Sharks can hear very low sounds, sometimes from more than a mile away. Sharks also have a keen sense of smell—some can detect one part of blood in a million parts of water to find prey, such as an injured seal. A shark can not only feel things that touch its skin, it can also "feel" movement in the water. A group of **vibration**-sensitive cells called the **lateral line** runs along the shark's sides and allow it to sense movement, like a school of fish.

Finally, sharks can see well in dim light. They have a mirrorlike layer of cells in the backs of their eyes that reflects light back into the rest of the eye. This lets them use as much light as possible to see. These cells also cause a shark's eyes to appear to glow in the dark, like a cat's.

SLICK SKIN

Sharks are covered with dermal denticles, which are tiny, toothlike scales. If you were to pet a shark (not a good idea!), its skin would feel smooth in one direction but rough, like sandpaper, in the other.

EXTRA SENSE

What are those "freckles" on many shark snouts? They are jelly-filled pores called ampullae of Lorenzini. These special pores allow sharks to sense electrical impulses created by other animals.

Caribbean reef shark

Divers fold their arms so they don't look threatening to the sharks.

THE INSIDE STORY

Sharks are built for swimming. Their **skeletons** are made of **cartilage**, which is lighter and more flexible than bone. And unlike most animals, a shark's muscles are not attached to its skeleton. Instead, the muscles are attached to its skin, which allows the shark to swim more efficiently. Sharks also have an extra-large liver that contains fatty oils. Because oil floats in water, the shark's liver makes its body more **buoyant** and makes swimming even easier.

These things are important because most sharks need to swim in order to breathe. As a shark swims, water flows through **gill slits** inside its mouth and over its **gills**. The gills remove **oxygen** from the water and add it to the shark's blood. The water then flows out through the five to seven gill slits visible on the shark's sides.

HOT OR COLD

The body temperature of most sharks is the same as the water around them. But some sharks, like threshers and great whites, can make their own heat, allowing them to be more active in colder waters.

Great white shark

Zebra shark

SINK OR SWIM

To get oxygen, most sharks swim with their mouths open, "ramming" water through their gills. This is called ram ventilation. Some sharks—like this zebra shark—can use their cheek muscles to force water over their gills instead.

MAKING MORE SHARKS

Shark **mating** is rarely seen in the wild. One thing we know is that male sharks hold on to females by biting their backs or pectoral fins during the process. Ouch! Luckily for females, their skin can be three times thicker than that of male sharks.

Unlike most fish, **fertilization** takes place inside the female's body. From there, the way a baby shark develops depends on the shark species. Some females lay fertilized eggs with tough outer cases in safe places. Other females keep the egg cases inside their bodies until the eggs hatch, giving birth to live young sharks called pups. Some shark pups grow inside the mother in an organ called the **uterus** instead of an egg case. Some females have two of these organs.

The number of pups a mother can have varies among sharks. As soon as all sharks are born, though, they must survive on their own.

A TOUGH CASE

The corners of a swell shark egg case have hooks or threads that anchor the case in place. The empty cases, which often wash up on beaches, are called mermaid's purses.

SIBLING RIVALRY

Sand tiger sharks give birth to two pups, one from each uterus. There are usually more pups after fertilization, but the two strongest pups eat the other pups during development.

Before mating, gray reef sharks gracefully swim around each other like ballet dancers.

Gray reef sharks

CATCH OF THE DAY

Sharks' senses help them track down their prey. But what sharks catch—and how they catch it—can be very different from species to species. Some, like the angel shark, hide themselves and **ambush** their prey. Others, like the nurse shark, prowl the sandy ocean floor searching for tasty crabs or squid. A few are filter-feeders that glide through the ocean with their mouths open, taking in tiny creatures such as plankton. Still others use speed to capture prey. A great white shark may sneak up on its prey from below, then attack with a lightning-fast vertical strike.

Most sharks feed alone, though a few may hunt in groups. When there is a large source of food, such as a school of fish, some sharks may engage in a feeding frenzy. The sharks will aggressively bite anything nearby—even each other!

Great white shark

SHARK TEETH

Shark teeth have different shapes depending on the shark's diet. Sand tigers have long, sharp teeth perfect for stabbing slippery fish. Great whites have triangular, sawlike teeth that rip chunks of flesh from their prey.

YOU ARE WHAT YOU EAT

What do California sea otters and horn sharks have in common? Both have pink skeletons from eating purple sea urchins!

TAIL TALES

A shark swims forward by moving its body and tail, or **caudal fin**, from side to side. Its two sets of side fins, the **pectoral** and **pelvic fins**, help the shark **maneuver** in the water. The **dorsal fins** on the top of the body keep the shark from flipping over.

One shark, the thresher shark, uses its tail for more than swimming. A thresher's tail makes up half of its body length, and is used while hunting. How? Large numbers of fish often swim together in schools. Usually there is safety in these numbers because it can be harder for a predator to pick out a single fish among a large group. But thresher sharks use their extra-long tails like whips to slap at a school of fish. This stuns and sometimes even kills some of the fish in the school. The thresher then spins around and eats its meal. The tail of the thresher shark is so powerful that it is one of the few sharks that can leap out of the water.

THE TAILS TELL ALL

Shark tails are divided into two parts, called lobes. Longer upper lobes, like those on tiger sharks, make it easier for the animal to maneuver. Faster-swimming sharks, like the great white, have lobes that are almost equal in size.

Great white

Tiger shark

Nurse shark

FAST AND SLOW

The shortfin mako can swim in short bursts at 40 miles per hour or more. The Greenland shark lives in icy Arctic waters and swims at just one mile per hour.

Thresher sharks can grow up to 20 feet long!

Common thresher shark

BLENDING IN

Sharks are excellent hunters, but not all are fast. To get a meal, slow-swimming sharks often ambush their prey. To do this, some sharks have skin coloring and patterns that help them blend into the background, which is called camouflage. Perhaps the best-camouflaged shark is the tasseled wobbegong. This bottom-feeding shark lives in coral reefs. It has **mottled** skin with a row of skin flaps, or fringe, around its nose and mouth. It looks just like a floating clump of plants or coral. But if an unwary fish happens by, the shark will quickly gulp down a meal.

Not all sharks use camouflage to catch dinner—some use it to avoid being dinner. Young zebra and tiger sharks are born with patterned skin coloring that helps them hide from larger sharks. As these sharks grow, the patterns will disappear.

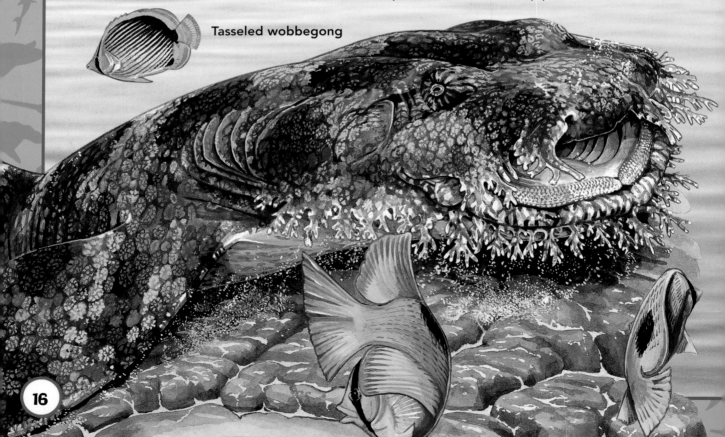

Tasseled wobbegong

SURPRISE!

Young nurse sharks will sometimes lie motionless on the ocean bottom and curl their pectoral fins to make a small "cave." If a crab wanders in looking for shelter, the shark has an easy meal.

TWO COLORS

Many sharks have dark backs and light bellies, which is known as counter-shading. This makes the shark hard to see from above, because its back blends with the darkness of the ocean. From below, its belly blends with the light at the surface.

Gray reef shark

HANGERS-ON

While most fish swim away from sharks, some creatures actually hitch rides with them. It turns out that tiny **parasites** live on sharks, feeding on the sharks' skin or blood. Luckily, other creatures help sharks by eating the parasites. One of these is the remora. The fish uses a small, flat disk on its head to attach itself to a shark using **suction**. In addition to a free ride, the remora eats pesky parasites off the shark and enjoys any scraps left over after the shark feeds.

Pilot fish also feed on scraps and parasites, helping the shark. But instead of attaching itself to the shark, the pilot fish "surfs" on the waves made by the shark as it swims through the water. The pilot fish must be careful, though, or it can wind up as a meal for the shark.

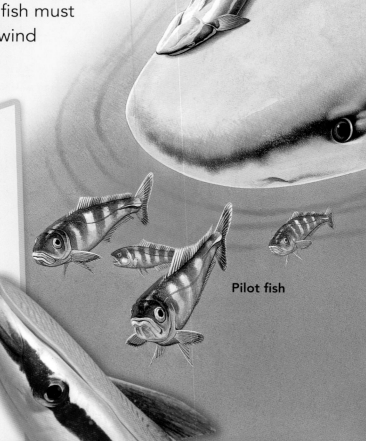

Remoras

Pilot fish

RIDE-ALONG REMORAS

Remoras will attach themselves to other large sea creatures, including whales, sea turtles, and manta rays. There are many species of remoras, and each has its own specific sea creature it prefers to ride with.

Sandbar sharks are considered to be one of the safest sharks to swim with. They rarely attack humans.

Sandbar shark

CLEANING STATIONS

A cleaning station is a bit like a fish beauty parlor. Sharks and other fish will swim through these areas so that creatures like the cleaning wrasse or the cleaner shrimp can dart up and eat the parasites on the skin of the fish. Because this helps both animals, their relationship is an example of **symbiosis**.

ALL IN THE FAMILY

You might not see the resemblance, but rays and skates are sharks' closest living relatives. Like sharks, rays and skates have skeletons made of cartilage instead of bone. But rays and skates have flattened bodies and large, winglike pectoral fins. They flap these large fins up and down like wings to push themselves through the water instead of using their tails as sharks do. The tails on rays and skates have other purposes—hunting or defense—and some tails are equipped with spikes or even **venomous** barbs.

Unlike sharks, these creatures have eyes on top of their heads and mouths on the bottom. This allows them to see what's swimming above them while hunting for food below. The largest of all the rays is the manta ray. It can grow to reach 22 feet from fin to fin!

SAWFISH

Sawfish, which are a type of ray, are equipped with long snouts that are studded with toothlike points. They use the special snout to dig up prey or to slash at a school of fish.

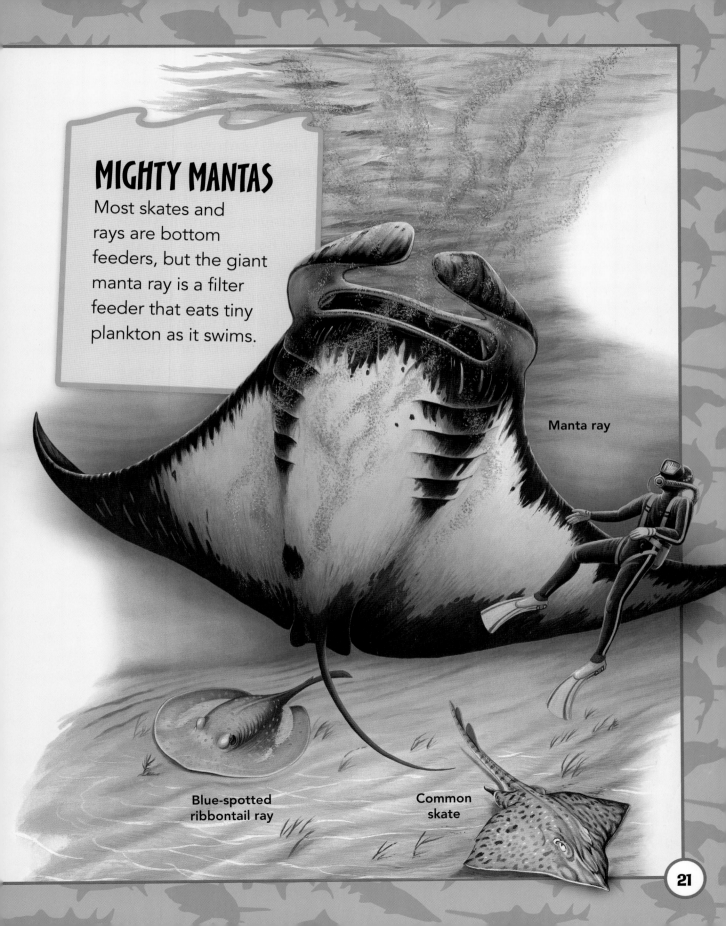

MIGHTY MANTAS

Most skates and rays are bottom feeders, but the giant manta ray is a filter feeder that eats tiny plankton as it swims.

Manta ray

Blue-spotted ribbontail ray

Common skate

LIFE ON THE REEF

Coral reefs are found in clear, warm waters and are important **ecosystems** for many kinds of marine life. Fish and other creatures are able to hide in the reef's cracks and crevices. Small fish and plants are eaten by larger fish, which are eaten by the top predators—the reef sharks.

There are several species of reef sharks. One of these is the whitetip reef shark, which spends its day hiding in caves formed by coral—often stacked together with other whitetip sharks. At night these sharks swim through the reef to hunt. Their tough skin protects the sharks from the sharp coral.

Another reef shark, the blacktip, is considered a shy shark. Divers can tell if it feels threatened, though, because it will form an *S* shape with its body and roll from side to side before striking.

ROCKS, PLANTS, OR ANIMALS?

A coral reef may look like a pile of rocks, but it is really a **colony** of tiny animals called hard coral **polyps**. They have hard outer skeletons that make the colony resemble a group of rocks. Soft coral polyps have flexible skeletons, making their colonies look more like plants.

WORKING TOGETHER

Blacktip reef sharks have been observed working together to round up, or herd, a school of fish against the shore to make feeding easier. Once the fish are trapped, the sharks grab them and slip back into the sea.

SHALLOW SHARKS

The shallow waters near coastlines can be dark or murky, but they still get enough sunlight for plants to thrive. Tall **kelp** forests, large beds of sea grass, and **mangrove** roots create special ecosystems for many kinds of sea life, including sharks.

The plants in the shallows give shark pups a place to hide from larger predators. Leopard sharks, for example, are born with a special patterning that camouflages them among the kelp. Young lemon sharks often hide among the roots of mangrove trees—an area that also lets them find food. These places also provide food for older sharks, because so many other creatures live in them. In fact, some very large sharks, such as the tiger, lemon, and bull shark, often prowl in shallow waters.

Bull sharks will sometimes swim far upriver to find prey.

SAFE AND SOUND

The shallows provide a safe place for the horn shark's egg case. It is shaped like a screw. The mother horn shark wedges it into a crack where it is hidden from prowling predators.

Green sea turtle

Bull shark

WHO SHARES THE SHALLOWS?

Sea otters, Garibaldi fish, and sea lions are among the creatures that live and hunt in the kelp forests of the world. Sea turtles, parrot fish, and manatees all graze on sea grass beds.

25

USING THEIR HEADS

Hammerhead sharks are probably the easiest sharks to recognize because of their unique head shapes. Their hammer-shaped heads are useful for hunting in the shallows, where it can be hard to locate hidden prey. The hammerhead's extra-wide snout allows it to have more electricity-sensing ampullae of Lorenzini, which it uses to locate creatures buried in the sand.

There are nine types of hammerhead sharks, and each has a head with a slightly different shape that helps it hunt. The great hammerhead, for example, uses its head to pin down rays, its favorite prey. Bonnetheads use their heads as shovels to dig up animals from the sandy ocean bottom.

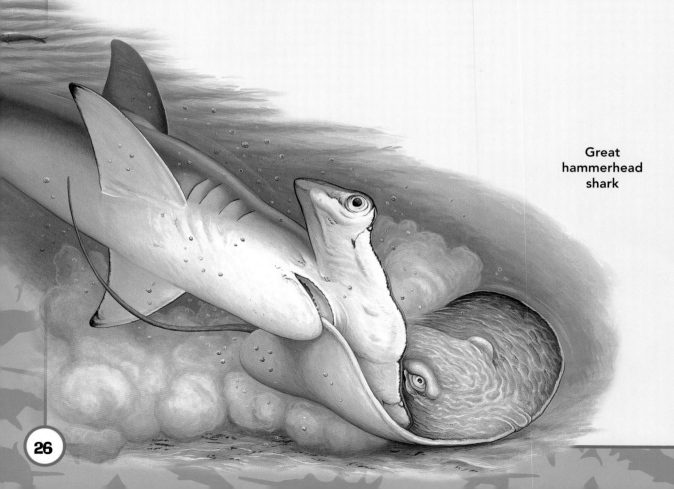

Great hammerhead shark

HAMMERHEAD HEADS

Because their eyes are located far apart, hammerheads have great vision on both sides, but they can't see straight ahead. To make up for this, the shark swings its head back and forth as it swims.

Scalloped hammerhead shark

GETTING A LIFT

The shape of its head also helps the hammerhead to swim. As the shark's tail pushes it forward, water rushes faster under the head than over it. This creates lift—just like an airplane wing does.

THE GREAT WHITE

Great white sharks are the largest fish predators in the ocean. How big are they? Most adults are 15 to 20 feet long. Though found in most of the world's oceans, great whites like cool coastal waters where they can find prey such as seals, sea lions, and young whales. These powerful swimmers are even known to leap out of the water to catch seals.

A great white's mouth is filled with about 300 sharp, **serrated** teeth, arranged in rows. Like other sharks, a great white's teeth are set into its gums instead of its jaws. That means teeth often fall out as the shark eats. Luckily for the great white and other sharks, when one tooth falls out, the one behind it moves up to take its place—as if it were on a conveyor belt.

BIG BATTLE

You might think the great white has no natural enemies. But orcas, also called killer whales, are bigger and faster than great whites and have been known to prey on them.

SHARK ATTACK

Considering how many hundreds of millions of people enter the ocean each year, shark attacks are relatively rare. It is more likely a person will be hit by lightning than be bitten by a shark.

A great white can take 20-pound chunks out of its prey!

GENTLE GIANTS

Several of the largest sharks eat some of the smallest creatures in the ocean. Though filter-feeding sharks have teeth, they don't use them to catch their food. Instead, sharks such as the whale shark and megamouth shark take in water as they swim. The seawater contains tiny creatures such as plankton, plants, and small fish.

Filter-feeders have comblike structures inside their mouths called **gill rakers**, which allow the shark to strain the food, like a sieve. After the water flows out through the shark's gill slits, the shark will swallow its food. How big are these sharks? The whale shark is the largest of all sharks and can grow to more than 40 feet long. Like basking sharks and megamouth sharks, whale sharks travel over long distances to find patches of water that are rich with food.

Whale shark

Scientists think some whale sharks may travel up to 9,000 miles in search of food.

OPEN WIDE

The whale and megamouth sharks can actively suck or pump water over their gill rakers, while the basking shark simply lets water flow into its open mouth as it swims.

BIG MOUTH

The megamouth shark lives deep in the ocean and only comes to the surface at night. Perhaps that's why it was not discovered until 1976, and it is still rarely seen today.

OUT IN THE OPEN

If you look at a map of the world, you will see that large parts of the ocean aren't near land at all. These areas, known as the open ocean, are home to animals living at different depths. Most animals live near the surface, where sunlight reaches the water. Sharks such as the blue, oceanic whitetip, and silky sharks use their incredible senses to find food, such as tuna or squid, in the open ocean.

The midwater area begins about 600 feet below the surface. There is very little sunlight here, and many animals survive by eating what drifts down from above. This unusual place is home to some strange-looking sharks, including the goblin shark and the frilled shark, which often prey on squid. In fact, it is said that the frilled shark may have inspired the legends of sea serpents.

Frilled sharks look a lot like fossilized sharks that lived 200 million years ago.

Frilled shark

Giant squid may release large ink clouds to confuse predators or prey.

Giant squid

SUPER SQUID

The rare giant squid may be as long as 60 feet with its tentacles outstretched, and each eye is about the size of a large pizza. It's possible that great whites prey on these huge creatures—but it's also possible that giant squid prey on the sharks!

JUST A BITE

The cookie-cutter shark lives in the midwaters, but heads to the surface to take small bites from larger creatures such as whales, dolphins, and other sharks.

MYSTERIES OF THE DEEP

The deeper you dive into the ocean, the darker and colder it gets. Yet even 3,000 feet below the surface, sharks are able to survive. Humans, however, cannot swim in these waters, because the pressure is too great. To explore here, scientists must use submarines or submersibles instead.

Fish have special adaptations to live in the deep. The lantern shark is one of the few sharks than can produce light. As it swims toward the surface to eat, its glowing belly helps it hide from predators lurking below. One of those predators is the gulper shark, which has large green eyes that can see even at great depths.

However, shark populations are declining worldwide. It is estimated that more than 100 million sharks are caught for food or sport each year, and some species may not recover. As we learn more about sharks, perhaps we can change the way we treat these fascinating fish.

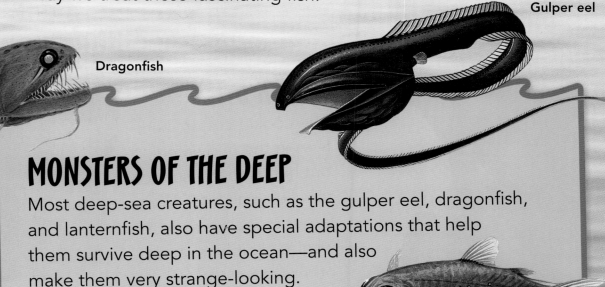

Gulper eel

Dragonfish

MONSTERS OF THE DEEP

Most deep-sea creatures, such as the gulper eel, dragonfish, and lanternfish, also have special adaptations that help them survive deep in the ocean—and also make them very strange-looking.

Lanternfish

SHINE BRIGHT

Some creatures that live in the dark depths make their own light, which is called bioluminescence. They sometimes use the light to attract prey, which may mistake the light for food. This photo shows bioluminescence of creatures on the shoreline.

Pygmy shark

Gulper sharks can be found two miles below the ocean's surface.

Gulper shark

GLOSSARY

adapt: to change in order to survive in a specific environment

ambush: a surprise attack by a hiding predator

buoyant: able to float in a liquid

cartilage: a tough, flexible tissue that is lighter than bone

caudal fin: the tail fin of a fish

colony: a grouping of similar individuals

dorsal fins: fins on the top of the fish that keep it from rolling over in the water

ecosystem: a group of interconnected plants and animals living in a specific environment

fertilization: the union of a sperm and an egg to create offspring

gill: an organ that removes oxygen from the water

gill rakers: comblike structures that strain food from the water

gill slits: the visible openings to the gills

kelp: large seaweed plants that grow in shallow ocean water

lateral line: a series of sense organs in a shark's sides that can feel movement in the water

maneuver: to move carefully around something

mangrove: a woody plant with large roots that grows in swamps and shallow water and can survive in salt water

mating: the act of coming together to produce offspring

mottled: spotted or blotchy

oxygen: a chemical found in air and water, and which most living organisms need to survive

parasite: an organism that survives by living and feeding on another plant or animal, called a host

pectoral fins: the front pair of fins on a fish's side, behind the gills; pectoral fins can provide "lift" like an airplane's wings as a fish swims forward, and also help it turn

pelvic fins: the back pair of fins on a fish's side, which keeps the fish stable and helps it move up and down

plankton: tiny plants and animals that drift in the ocean

polyp: the living part of a coral; when the polyp dies, it leaves behind a chalky skeleton

predator: an animal that hunts other creatures for food

prey: an animal that is hunted by another animal

serrated: having notches along an edge

skeleton: the supporting structure of an organism; it can be inside or outside of a creature's body

species: closely related plants or animals that can produce offspring

suction: the removal of water or air that results in a change in pressure and allows something to stick to a surface

symbiosis: two species whose close physical interactions benefit both species

uterus: an organ inside a female animal in which the young develop

venomous: able to inject poison

vibration: the act of moving back and forth quickly in a rhythmic pattern

3-D MODEL INSTRUCTIONS

Complete one model at a time. Press out the pieces and arrange them as shown. Using the numbers on the pictures here, match the slots and assemble your 3-D ocean animals.

GREAT WHITE SHARK

Like most sharks, great whites have powerful bites. Their jaws can slide out of their mouths as they attack, giving them extra force.

MANTA RAY

Large manta rays can measure 22 feet from fin to fin—about four times the height of an average adult human.

HAMMERHEAD SHARK

Great hammerhead sharks can grow to 20 feet long.

WHALE SHARK

The whale shark is the size of a school bus, but it eats tiny creatures such as plankton and krill.

DIORAMA INSTRUCTIONS

Bring your own ocean world to life by building a beautiful diorama. It's easy!

1. The inside of the box lid and base will be the walls of your diorama. The unfolding board will be the floor. Decorate these with reusable stickers as desired.

2. Press out the floor figures, and fold as shown. Decorate with stickers if desired. Fold, then slide the rectangular tabs through the floor slots, folding them underneath so the figures stand upright. The tabs and slots are all the same size, so you can change the position of the figures.

3. Stand the box lid and base upright and at an angle as shown. Lay the angled back edges of the floor piece on top of the box sides. You're done!

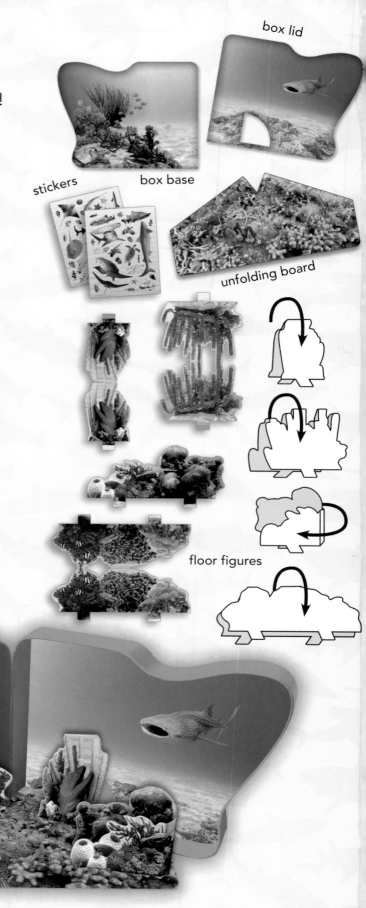

box lid

box base

stickers

unfolding board

floor figures